# William's Day Off and Other Stories

Richmal Crompton, who wrote the original *Just William* stories, was born in Lancashire in 1890. The first story about William Brown appeared in *Home* magazine in 1919, and the first collection of William stories was published in book form three years later. In all, thirty-eight William books were published, the last one in 1970, after Richmal Crompton's death.

Martin Jarvis, who has adapted the stories in this book for younger readers, first discovered *Just William* when he was nine years old. He made his first adaptation of a William story for BBC radio in 1973 and since then his broadcast readings have become classics in their own right. BBC Worldwide have released nearly a hundred William stories on audio cassette and for these international best-sellers Martin has received a Gold Disc and the British Talkies Award. An award-winning actor, Martin has also appeared in numerous stage plays, television series and films.

**Titles in the *Meet Just William* series**

William's Birthday and Other Stories
William and the Hidden Treasure and Other Stories
William's Wonderful Plan and Other Stories
William and the Prize Cat and Other Stories
William and the Haunted House and Other Stories
William's Day Off and Other Stories

# William's Day Off and Other Stories

Adapted from Richmal Crompton's
original stories by Martin Jarvis

Illustrated by Tony Ross

MACMILLAN CHILDREN'S BOOKS

First published 1999 by Macmillan Children's Books
a division of Macmillan Publishers Limited
20 New Wharf Road, London N1 9RR
Basingstoke and Oxford
www.panmacmillan.com

Associated companies throughout the world

ISBN 0 330 39099 6



7 9 8 6

A CIP catalogue record for this book is available from the British Library.

Typeset by SX Composing DTP, Rayleigh, Essex
Printed and bound in Great Britain by Mackays of Chatham plc, Kent

# Contents

Dear Reader

Ullo. I'm William Brown. Spect you've heard of me an' my dog Jumble cause we're jolly famous on account of all the adventures wot me an' my friends the Outlaws have.

Me an' the Outlaws try an' avoid our famlies cause they don' unnerstan' us. Specially my big brother Robert an' my rotten sister Ethel. She's awful. An' my parents are really <u>hartless</u>. Y'know, my father stops my pocket-money for no reason at all, an' my mother never lets me keep pet rats or <u>anythin'</u>.

It's jolly hard bein' an Outlaw an' havin' adventures when no one unnerstan's you, I can tell you.

You can read all about me, if you like, in this excitin' an' speshul new collexion of all my fav'rite stories. I hope you have a jolly gud time readin' 'em.

Yours truly

William Brown

# William's Day Off

"They're slum children from London," said Ginger. "They've come for four days. They've never seen a cow, or anything like that."

"Well, there's not much to see in a cow," said William. "You can't have any fun with a cow. I've tried. Where did you say they were comin'?"

"To Eastbrook Farm. Mrs Camp's havin' 'em. They're sent by some sort of soci'ty what pays for slum children to come into the country, 'cause of the war."

"Well, I vote we take 'em round a bit, and show 'em woods an' cows an' things," said William.

"Miss Milton's sister's havin' 'em to tea

'safternoon," put in Henry. "I heard my mother say so this mornin'."

"Corks!" said William, aghast. "Fancy them havin' to waste an afternoon goin' to *her*."

Miss Milton had lent her cottage to her sister for the summer, and though William had not yet met the lady, he had received the discouraging news that she was almost an exact replica of her sister.

Next morning the Outlaws went over to Eastbrook Farm. They found two boys standing by the farm gate wearing grey shorts and grey jerseys. They looked very clean and very bored.

The newcomers it turned out were called Bert and Syd. They were ten and eleven years old.

No, they didn't think much of the country so far. A goat had butted them, and a gander had chased them. They were obviously disillusioned and homesick.

"You come along with us," suggested

William, "an' we'll show you some of our places."

"Don't mind if we do," agreed Bert cautiously.

Bert was the elder. He had a slight cast in one eye that lent him a slightly sardonic aspect, and a more than slight suggestion of adenoids.

Syd was small and gingery and obviously ready to follow Bert's lead unquestioningly.

"Don't mind if we do," Syd repeated.

They accompanied the Outlaws to the old barn, and any hostilities soon melted in the warmth of the Outlaws' friendliness. Two hours later, the six returned to the farm, firm friends.

"Tell you what we'll do this afternoon," said William. "We'll go over to Marleigh. There's some caves there an' we can play smugglers."

"Coo," said Bert regretfully, "I don't 'arf wish we could, but we can't. We've gotter go to tea somewhere this afternoon."

"A Miss Milton or somethin'," supplemented Syd.

"Huh, you'll have a jolly dull time there," William prophesied. "She's *awful.*"

"She won't even give you a decent tea, if she's anythin' like her sister," said Ginger.

"She's worse then her sister," said Douglas gloomily. "I've seen her."

"Yes, but Mrs Camp'll make us go, I expect," said Bert.

All eyes turned to William.

"I say," he began, "s'pose two of us pretend to be Bert and Syd and go to tea at old Miss Milton's 'stead of them. It doesn't much matter for us, 'cause we can go to Marleigh Caves any day, but they've only got four days and it might rain on the others."

"She's seen me," said Ginger.

"And me," said Henry and Douglas.

"But she's *not* seen me," said William. "Tell you what. I'll say I'm Bert and that Syd's gotter cold or somethin', and then you can all go off to Marleigh Caves, and I'll go 'n' have tea with her, an' she'll never know it's not you."

"Coo," said Bert. "That's jolly decent of yer."

"Not 'arf," agreed Syd.

"Are you *sure* she's not seen you?" said Ginger.

"'Course I'm sure," said William. "And anyway, I'll make myself look different, same as actors and detectives do. Right then. We'll all meet at the ole barn, an' you an' me'll change clothes, Bert. And you can go to Marleigh Caves."

"Good egg!" cried Bert and Syd simultaneously.

William walked purposefully towards Miss Milton's house, intent upon the manipulation of his face.

He was representing Bert's slight cast by his best squint. Bert's suggestion of adenoids he represented by opening his mouth loosely to the size of a ping-pong ball.

In order further to disguise himself, he had damped his hair and brushed it into a straight fringe, and was walking with a curious, stooping, shambling gait, letting his hands dangle about his knees.

Miss Milton blenched slightly as she opened the front door.

"Please, ma'am," began William in a deep throaty voice. "Please, ma'am, I'm Bert, and Syd couldn't come. He's gotta bad cold."

He opened his eyes to their utmost

capacity, and fixed them on the end of his nose. He was finding his squint useful. It saved him from the necessity of meeting Miss Milton's eye.

"I'm sorry to hear that," said Miss Milton, conscientiously trying to overcome the distaste that his appearance inspired in her. Come in, dear boy. Wipe your feet well on the mat."

William followed her into the drawing room and sat down on a small chair by the window. Miss Milton looked at him, blinked, looked away, then, summoning all her courage, looked at him again.

"Are you enjoying your holiday in the country?" she said.

"Yes, ma'am," said William.

"I suppose you've never been in the country before, have you?"

"No, ma'am."

"It must be a delightful experience for you."

"Yes, ma'am."

"I hope you realise that you're a very lucky boy."

"Yes, ma'am."

Miss Milton tried to think of something else to say, but failed.

"Perhaps," she said at last, "you'd like to come out and see my sister's garden, would you?"

"Yes, ma'am," said William. He followed her out into the little garden.

"Now don't go on the grass," said Miss

Milton. "There's plenty of room for you to walk on the path."

William was tired of saying "Yes, ma'am". He was artist enough to want to make more of his part than that.

"Grass, ma'am?" he said, in his deep throaty voice. "What's grass?"

Miss Milton was taken aback. Surely even slum children knew what grass was? But evidently they didn't. So she hastened to explain.

"That's grass," she said, pointing to her sister's sparse little lawn. "It's – well, it's just grass."

William began to feel that a certain amount of enjoyment might, after all, be extracted from the situation. He pointed over the hedge to a cow in the next field.

"What's that?"

"Why, that's a cow."

"What's a cow?"

Miss Milton sighed. But of course, it was quite natural that a slum child should never have seen a cow.

"It's – er – it's just a cow, dear. A cow is – it's just a cow."

Miss Milton's cat sauntered out of the kitchen door, and eyed William sardonically.

"What's that?" he said.

"A cat, of course," said Miss Milton rather sharply. "Surely you've seen cats at home?"

William realised that he was rather over-doing his town-bred ignorance.

"It's bigger than town cats," he said hastily.

The cat, who had recognised William, winked at him, and went indoors again. William thought wistfully of Marleigh Caves and wished that he was there with the others.

"And now, dear, it's time we went in to tea."

William resisted the temptation to say, "What's tea?" and followed her into the dining room.

It was, as Ginger had prophesied, a rotten tea. William soon emptied the plates, but Miss Milton did not have them refilled.

She looked at him. "I suppose you've seen an oculist about your – erm – squint?"

"Er – yes," said William hastily, doing it again. "It comes on worse when I'm hungry."

"But you've just had your tea."

William made no comment on this.

"Well, just stay here a moment," said Miss Milton. "I'll try and get a little companion of your own age. You'd like that, wouldn't you?"

William grunted non-committally and she went into the hall. He followed her to the door to listen. She was telephoning to Mrs Lane.

Two minutes later, William saw his sworn enemy, Hubert Lane, entering the garden gate. Escape was impossible. He sat there intensifying his squint and opening his mouth to the size of a cricket ball.

Miss Milton went to the door and returned followed by Hubert. Hubert looked at William and recognition leapt into his eyes, then died away again.

The boy had looked like William Brown at first sight, but on further inspection he obviously wasn't. His clothes were different; his mouth was different; his eyes were different.

"This is Bert," Miss Milton introduced him. "And this, Bert, is Hubert. Now, Hubert, I want you to take Bert on a nice quiet walk down the road and show him the country. You'll go with Hubert, won't you, Bert?"

"Yes, ma'am," said William.

His voice was different too, thought Hubert.

"Come back in a quarter of an hour," Miss

Milton called after them as they set off down the road.

"I say, Bert," said Hubert, "you're awfully like a boy I know called William Brown. I mean, you are just at first. He's an awful boy. My mother won't let me play with him. I jolly well scored one off him today. I'm sellin' some piebald mice, shillin' each, and he wants one and I won't sell him one. And he's as mad as mad. I say, I've got a jolly good idea—"

They were passing William's house, and Hubert stopped.

"—Let's play a trick on him. You go in and go round to the back and smash the window in the tool-shed. I heard his father sayin' that the next time he broke that window, he wouldn't have any pocket money for a month. It's a jolly good trick, isn't it? Go on, go on. Do it quick and then come out. I'll wait for you here. Go on."

William crept round the back of the house, watched by the sniggering Hubert.

Then, out of sight, he entered the back door, slipped upstairs, changed into one of his ordinary suits, brushed his hair back, and came out of the front door with his usual sturdy tread, whistling, his hands in his pockets.

Hubert, still crouching behind the hedge, did not see William until he was almost upon him.

"Oh, hullo, Hubert," said William. "What are you doing here?"

Hubert blinked, gasped, and looked wildly at the path down which he'd seen Bert disappear.

"Er – um – I say, William, there's a – er – a boy in your back garden. I was just taking him for a walk and he ran away from me down into your back garden. I – I – told him not to. I hope he's not doin' any damage."

"Oh, I'll go and have a look for him," offered William cheerfully, and set off down the path.

He returned almost immediately.

"There's no one there. Who did you say it was?"

"He must be there. He's a country holiday boy called Bert. He'd gone to tea at Miss Milton's, and I was just taking him on a nice quiet walk down the road when he suddenly ran in at your gate. I don't know why. I called out, 'Come back', but he went on. I say, do you mind if I come round an' look for him."

"No, come on and have a look."

Hubert peered nervously into the tool-shed and the summer-house, followed by the grinning William.

"He – he can't have gone anywhere else, can he?" said Hubert distractedly. "I don't know what I'm goin' to do if I don't find him."

"He might've fallen into the rain tub an' got drowned," said William helpfully.

Hubert's face turned pale green. "What am I going to do? I can't go back to Miss Milton's without him. And I can't just go home because she'll ring up my mother and there'll be an awful fuss. I say, William, you will help me, won't you? I've got an idea. This boy was a bit like you. Jus' a bit. If you can sort of cross your eyes and hang your mouth open a bit, an' walk sort of doubled up, she might think it was him. I bet Miss Milton's jolly short-sighted. People like her always are."

"But what about clothes?" said William.

Hubert's face fell, then lit up again.

"You could put on your raincoat, and I could say that it looked like rain so we called at the farm for your raincoat, and she won't notice you've not got the same things underneath."

William considered, and then a light beamed suddenly in his eye, too.

"All right, I will, if you'll sell me one of your piebald mice."

Hubert hesitated. He had widely advertised his refusal to sell the mouse to William, and he would lose considerable face if he did so, but the crisis was an urgent one.

"Very well," he said.

"Here's the shillin'," said William. "You can go and fetch it now, and then I'll go with you to ole Miss Milton."

A few minutes later, William was hiding his piebald mouse carefully in a wooden box, with holes bored in for ventilation.

"Now, what d'you say this boy looked like?" he said in a businesslike tone, as he came out doing up the buttons of his raincoat.

"Well, he had a sort of squint, same as I told you."

William did a mild and tentative squint.

"What else?"

"His mouth sort of kept open all the time."

William opened his mouth to about the size of a ha'penny marble.

"Well, yes. I mean, it's jolly good. It's not *quite* like him, of course, but I bet she won't notice."

"Well, what do you want me to do? I've not got much time."

"Jus' come back to her with me and say you've had a jolly nice walk with me an' that sort of thing. An' that it's time you went home now. An' then go off down the road, as if you were going to Eastbrook Farm. An' then, if they say that this Bert never got home, she can't say it's my fault."

They walked down the road. Hubert's face grew paler as they approached Miss Milton's. The front door was open and Miss Milton was telephoning in the hall. She was evidently describing her guest to an acquaintance.

"Oh, he's just come in now," she said. "Hmm – he looks better already. Yes, come straight round. You have a little boy of your own, haven't you? Could he come too? Oh, he's out. Well, yes, I quite understand. But *you'll* come, won't you? You must of course be prepared for something very different from your own child."

She turned from the telephone to greet them.

"Well, dears."

William, with his modified squint, said that it was time he went home. Miss Milton, however, insisted on hearing a detailed account of their walk before he went.

"I suppose it opened a new world to you, didn't it, my boy?" she said to William.

Suddenly she looked out of the window.

"Oh, here's a lady who's kindly coming to see you, Bert," she said. "I'll just go and open the door."

They heard greetings in the hall, then the door was thrown open and, "This is Bert," said Miss Milton, pointing to him in a proprietary fashion.

William squinted wildly and opened his mouth almost to the size of a football, but in vain.

"*William!*" said Mrs Brown.

"'S not William," protested Hubert vehemently. "Honest. 'S not William. He's like William, but he's not William. It's Bert."

"Of course it's William," said Mrs Brown indignantly.

Hubert persisted that it was not William, and Miss Milton supported him. Mrs Brown said that a woman knew her own son after eleven years. William continued to squint and said nothing.

Then the real Bert, hot and breathless and dirty and gloriously happy, arrived. He'd had a wonderful afternoon at Marleigh, but on the way home had run into Mrs Camp who, discovering that he was wearing another boy's suit, had sent him to retrieve his jersey.

The altercation waxed fast and furious. Mrs Brown said that she knew nothing about Bert; all she knew was that William was William. Everyone talked at once, except William.

William waited patiently for the hubbub to subside. He'd have to give an account of himself soon enough. No need to precipitate matters.

Meantime, he was fixing his thoughts on the one bright spot in the whole situation. And the one bright spot in the whole situation was – the piebald mouse. Bert, or no Bert, that, at any rate, was safely his.

# William's Goodbye Present

"Uncle Paul's goin' back to Australia tomorrow," said Hubert Lane. "I'm goin' to see him off at Hadley Station. He says he'll call round an' say goodbye to you on the way."

"All right," said William amicably.

There had been a lull in the hostilities between the Hubert Laneites and the Outlaws during the visit of Hubert's Uncle Paul from Australia.

For Uncle Paul was an uncle after the Outlaws' own heart, and he evidently much preferred the Outlaws to his own nephew and his nephew's friends.

To William, the visit opened up whole new worlds of adventure, and he had proved an apt pupil at whistle and boat making.

In fact, Uncle Paul had said that the last boat William had made was almost as good as he could have made himself.

"Now, what you want," he said, "is a good knife. I'll give you one before I go. I'll get you one like mine if I can."

"Like yours!" gasped William incredulously.

"Yes," said Uncle Paul, glancing carelessly at the magnificent weapon with which he had just fashioned a perfectly formed and perfectly balanced boat. "Those little penknives of yours are no good."

The next day he had said, "I've not forgotten that claspknife of yours. I went into Hadley about it, and they hadn't one in stock, but they're going to get one."

On the last morning of Uncle Paul's visit William was hanging about his front gate when the car containing Uncle Paul and

Hubert came down the road on its way to Hadley station.

Uncle Paul stopped the car and jumped out.

"I was coming to see you to say goodbye," he said to William. "We've had a great time together, haven't we? Don't forget what I told you about lighting fires. And when you're tracking down wild animals be sure you're the right way of the wind or they'll get your scent. Oh, and about your knife—"

"Yes?" said William eagerly.

"They said they'd have it in first thing this morning, so I'll stop the car at the shop in Hadley and get it, and Hubert here can bring it back to you. That'll be all right, won't it?"

"Yes," agreed William heartily, "an' I'm jolly grateful to you. I've wanted a knife like that all my life."

"Splendid!" said Uncle Paul. "I'm giving Hubert a pistol for his present – Well, goodbye. See you again next time I'm over."

He drove off, Hubert sitting beside him with a faint secret smile on his face.

William's sorrow at the departure of Uncle Paul was mingled with joy at the prospect of the possession of the magnificent claspknife.

But the morning passed by and Hubert did not appear with the claspknife. After lunch, William could restrain his impatience no longer and set out for the Lanes' house.

Mrs Lane greeted him without enthusiasm. She was tired of seeing him about the place. Paul had encouraged him too much.

"Well?" she said coldly. "What do you want?"

"I've come for my knife," said William simply.

"Your *what*?" she said.

"My knife," said William. "The knife that Hubert's Uncle Paul's given Hubert for me."

"I don't know what you're talking about," said Mrs Lane. "Hubert had a knife that his Uncle Paul gave him for a parting present, but I know nothing about any knife of yours. Hubert!" she called.

Hubert came slowly into the hall. His fat, pale face still wore the faint smile.

"I've come for my knife," said William sternly.

The smile spread all over Hubert's fat, pale face. "What knife?" he said.

"The knife Uncle Paul said he was giving you for me."

Hubert took from his pocket an exact, but shiningly new, replica of Uncle Paul's claspknife.

"Yes, that's it," said William eagerly.

But Hubert did not at once hand it over with apologies for the delay.

Instead, he slipped it back into his pocket with a careless air of proprietorship.

"That's my knife," he said. "He gave it me for a goodbye present."

"He said he was giving you a pistol for a goodbye present," said William indignantly.

Hubert took out a shining new pistol from another pocket.

"Yes," he smiled. "He gave me that, too."

William gazed at him blankly.

"But he *promised* the knife to me. You were there when he did. He said he'd call at the shop for it and give it you to give to me."

"He never did," said Hubert. "He never said anything about a knife when he called to say goodbye to you. He gave this knife to me. That's all I know."

William was, for a moment, struck speechless with horror. He turned indignantly to Mrs Lane.

"It *is* my knife," he said. "Uncle Paul told me he was going to give it to me. He was goin' to call for it in Hadley this mornin', and give it to Hubert to give to me. He told me so. Hubert was there when he told me so."

Mrs Lane looked at Hubert.

"Did he, Hubert?"

Hubert met her eye blandly.

"'Course he didn't," he said. "He's jus' makin' it all up to get the claspknife off me."

William stared at him.

"You *naughty* boy!" Mrs Lane was saying. "How *dare* you come here with a string of lies like this?"

"But he did," said William desperately.

"Be quiet. Go away at once, William Brown."

William knew that further protestation would be useless.

Stunned and bewildered, he walked gloomily to the old barn where he had arranged to meet the Outlaws, to show them his precious new possession. As soon as they saw him they knew that something was wrong.

Not thus – slowly, dejectedly, thoughtfully – does the owner of a brand new claspknife walk.

"Haven't you got it?" called Ginger as he approached.

"No," said William.

"Never mind," said Ginger. "I bet it'll have come before tonight."

"Oh, it's come," said William bitterly. "It's come all right."

They stared at him in astonishment. Why wasn't he swaggering, then? Why wasn't he displaying it?

"Where is it, then?" demanded Douglas.

"*He's* got it," said William.

"Who?"

"Hubert Lane," said William, spitting the name out as if it were some noxious draught.

They crowded round him in consternation as he told them the whole story.

Hubert, of course, had no real use for the claspknife. He was definitely not a claspknife boy.

He had taken so much trouble to obtain it only because William wanted it and he wanted to "score off" William. The pleasure he got out of it was in hanging out of his bedroom window, safe from attack, and displaying it to William and the Outlaws with jeering triumph whenever they passed down the road in front of his house.

It was just when William had almost given up hope of either getting back his knife or avenging the insult that an idea occurred to him. He remembered quite suddenly the weak spot in Hubert's armour. Hubert still believed in fairies and witches and spells.

There had been an historic occasion when he had even managed to persuade Hubert that he had been made invisible. Surely that weakness could be turned to account now?

He called a meeting of the Outlaws in the old barn, and together they formed a Plan.

The next morning William and Ginger stood in the road, in front of the Lanes' house.

William, assuming a nauseatingly pleasant expression, called up to Hubert's window, "Will you come out an' play with us, Hubert?"

Hubert appeared at his bedroom window. Ginger imitated William's nauseous expression.

"Come and play with us, Hubert," pleaded

Ginger. "It's all right. We've got a secret. We've not told anyone else yet. We'll tell you if you'll come."

Next to greed, Hubert's consuming passion was curiosity. They knew that he would now have no peace of mind till he had learnt the secret.

"All right," he said condescendingly. "I'll come along."

He vanished from the window and soon appeared at the gate.

"It's all right about that knife, Hubert," said William. "You can keep it."

"Thought you'd feel that way," said Hubert with an unpleasant sneer. He took out the knife from one pocket, the pistol from another, flourished them carelessly then restored them to his pockets.

The two Outlaws restrained themselves. They walked together until they reached the field by the old barn. William and Ginger led Hubert across the stile into the field.

"Well," said Hubert, "what's this secret of yours?"

"It's this," said William, lowering his voice. "When we came here this morning, we saw an ole woman in the field, with a cloak an' a big pointed hat an' a broomstick."

The superior sneer fell from Hubert's face.

"It was a witch," he said. "It was a witch, of course. What was she doin'?"

"She was jus' goin' about an' wavin' her broomstick an' sayin' things."

"Spells!" said Hubert, his round, credulous face pink with eagerness. "She was makin' spells. I say" – his eyes glinted greedily – "did she say anythin' about findin' treasure or anythin' like that?"

Walking by his side, William carefully led Hubert on to a spot that had recently been burnt brown by one of the Outlaws' camp-fires.

"She said somethin' over that bit you're walkin' on now," he said reflectively.

"What was it?" said Hubert.

"Well, it went somethin' like this," said William:

*"Whoever treads upon this bit of burned,*
*Into a hen-coop shall his home be turned.*

"And then it went on, somethin' about all the family that was in the house should be turned into hens an' anyone of the family who wasn't in it when the spell came on should be turned into hens the minute they saw the hen-coop."

Hubert's mouth dropped open and he leapt quickly away from the patch of burnt grass.

"W-w-w-what? A hen-coop?"

"Yes," said William, "but I don't suppose there's really anythin' in it. Go'n look if your house is turned into a hen-coop. You can see it from the stile, can't you?"

Hubert started forward, then remembered the second part of the spell, and returned.

"I'd better not," he said anxiously. "You go 'n' look," he added, turning to Ginger.

Ginger went down to the stile, from which he could see the solid four-square structure of stone and brick that was the Lanes' house.

"Crumbs!" he shouted in well-simulated horror. "It's gone. There's only a hen-coop."

Hubert paled.

"I don't b'lieve you; I d-d-d-don't believe you."

"Well, come and look for yourself," challenged Ginger.

Again Hubert remembered the latter part of the spell, and shook his head.

"No, I won't," he said. "You want to get me turned into a hen, that's what you want. Anyway, I don't believe you."

"Well, come and look for yourself if you don't believe me."

Matters having thus reached a deadlock, Douglas appeared, sauntering idly from behind the old barn.

"I say, Hubert," said Douglas airily, "what's happened to your house?"

"W-w-w-what?"

"It's gone," said Douglas. "I've just passed it now, an' it's gone, an' there's a hen-coop where it was, with a brown an' white hen scratchin' about outside it."

That was a clever touch of verisimilitude on Douglas's part. He had seen Mrs Lane through the window and she had been wearing a brown and white dress.

"Corks! That'll be Mother," said Hubert.

"I say, there's a hen jus' setting off from the coop an' going down the road," called Ginger from the stile.

"That'll be Father," moaned Hubert. "He goes to the station about this time."

"I bet they won't let him on the train," said Ginger. "Not like that."

Henry appeared suddenly in the road and vaulted the stile.

"I say!" he said. "Hubert's house has gone. "There's jus' a hen-coop there."

At this proof from yet another independent source, Hubert burst into tears. They crowded round, comforting him.

"Don't worry, Hubert. They have quite a good time, hens."

"You'll get to like worms an' grubs after a bit, I expect."

"You'd better go back an' get turned into one now an' get it over. You'll get used to it."

"I expect you're hungry aren't you, Hubert? You'd better go home an' have some nice grubs an' worms.

"I bet you'll get a bit tired at first, havin' to sleep on one leg, but it won't seem so bad after a year or two."

"I believe he's turning into one now, don't you? His face is gettin' jus' like a hen's."

Hubert's sobs turned into long howls.

"I d-d-don't want to be a h-h-h-hen, I d-d-d-don't want to be a h-h-h-hen."

"Well, listen, Hubert," said William kindly. "I heard this witch say somethin' else, after she'd said about the hens."

"W-what did she say?"

"Well," said William, "she went over to the stream here – an' she waved her broomstick over it an' she said:

*"An' never shall he be free of the spell*
*Till he throws into here somethin' that cuts*
*an' somethin' that shoots as well."*

Hubert blinked and considered. Then he plunged his hand into his pocket and brought out the claspknife.

"D'you think that'd do?" he said anxiously.

William examined it with a judicial air.

"It might," he said. "It cuts, anyway. No harm in tryin'. But what about the other? She said, 'Somethin' that shoots as well'."

From another pocket Hubert brought out his pistol.

"What about this? Would this do?"

"You might try," said William doubtfully. "Try throwin' 'em both in together—"

Pistol and penknife fell with a splash into the little stream. At once Ginger raised a cry from the stile.

"I say! Hubert's house has come back. That hen-coop's gone, an' Hubert's house has come back."

Hubert's fat, tear-stained face shone with relief.

"Corks!" he said. "I'm jolly glad you heard her say that end bit."

"She said somethin' else," said William. "She said that if ever you came here to look for 'em in the stream or if ever you told anyone about this hen business, you'd be turned into somethin' a jolly sight worse than a hen."

Hubert paled again.

"I won't," he said earnestly. "I jolly well won't – I promise I won't – I say! I don't look as if I'm turnin' into a hen now, do I?"

"No," William reassured him. "You're gone quite back to a boy again now."

Cautiously, fearfully, Hubert approached the stile. Then he gave a whoop of joy. "It *has* come back! It's all right. It has come back."

"Well, don't you forget about not tellin' anyone," William warned him.

"No, I won't," said Hubert fervently, "and I'm jolly grateful to you for remembering the end part, the part that turned it back. Worms!

I was jolly well dreadin' having to eat worms. Well, I'm goin' home, then, I'm jolly hungry. Worms!" he said again. "Ugh!" And he set off at his fat, slow trot, down the road towards the house.

The next morning, the Outlaws passed Hubert as he was standing at the gate. William held the claspknife and Ginger the pistol. Neither had been damaged by its brief immersion in the stream.

Hubert looked at them with interest. "Where did you get those?" he said.

William turned a bland, expressionless face to him. "The fairies gave them us," he said.

# William Plays Santa Claus

William walked slowly and thoughtfully down the village street. It was the week after Christmas. Suddenly he saw someone coming towards him.

It was Mr Solomon, the superintendent of the Sunday school of which William was a reluctant member.

William had just heard that Mr Solomon was going to form a band from the elder boys of the Sunday school.

William confronted him.

"Afternoon, Mr Solomon," he said.

Mr Solomon looked him up and down with distaste.

"Good afternoon, my boy," he said icily. "I am on my way to pay a visit to your parents."

This news was not encouraging.

William turned to accompany him and boldly broached the subject of the band.

"Hear you're gettin' up a band, Mr Solomon," he said casually.

"I am," said Mr Solomon, more icily than ever.

"I'd like to be a trumpeter," said William, still casually.

"You have not been asked to join the band," went on Mr Solomon, "and you will *not* be asked to join the band."

"Oh," said William politely.

They walked on.

"I am going," continued Mr Solomon, "to complain to your parents of your shameful behaviour on Christmas Eve, when you were supposed to be carol-singing."

"Oh – that," said William as though he remembered the incident with difficulty. "I remember – we . . . sort of lost you, didn't we?"

He and the Outlaws had, in fact, spent the evening in glorious lawlessness.

Mr Solomon turned in at the gate of William's home, and William accompanied him with an air of courage that was derived solely from the knowledge that both his parents were out.

He went round to the side of the house. His companion went up the front steps, rang the bell, and was invited in to tea by Ethel, William's grown-up sister.

William had forgotten that Ethel was at home, nursing a cold.

Ethel happened to be in the temporary and, for her, very rare position of being without a male admirer on the spot. Everyone seemed to have gone away for Christmas.

Mr Solomon was not, of course, a victim worthy of Ethel's bow and spear, but he was better than no one. Therefore she gave him tea and smiled upon him.

He sat, blushing deeply and gazing in rapt adoration at her blue eyes and Titian red hair.

He had not even dared to tell her the *real* object of his visit lest it should prejudice her against him.

William went indoors, assumed his most guileless expression, and entered the drawing-room. He sat down upon a chair next to Mr Solomon.

After a silence Ethel spoke without enthusiasm.

"Mr Solomon has very kindly come to make sure that you're none the worse after your little outing on Christmas Eve."

William turned his gaze upon Mr Solomon. Mr Solomon went pink and nearly choked over his tea.

Demoralised by Ethel's beauty and sweetness of manner he had indeed substituted for his intended complaint a kindly enquiry as to William's health.

William made no comment.

"That's very kind of him, isn't it, William?" said Ethel rather sharply. "You ought to thank him."

"Thank you," he said in a tone in which Mr Solomon perceived quite plainly mockery and scorn.

Another silence fell. Suddenly the clock struck five and Mr Solomon started up.

"Good heavens!" he said. "I must go. I ought to have been there by five."

"Where?" said Ethel.

"At the school. It's the old folks' Christmas party. I was to give out the presents – the mixed infants' party too – I'm afraid I shall be terribly late."

He looked about frantically.

"Oh, but can't someone else do it for you?" said Ethel. "It seems such a shame for you to have to run off as soon as you've come."

Mr Solomon looked into Ethel's blue, blue eyes and was lost.

He didn't care who gave away the presents to the old folks and the mixed infants. He didn't care whether anyone gave them away. All he wanted to do was to sit in this room and be smiled upon by Ethel.

It came to him suddenly that he'd met his soulmate at last.

"Isn't there anyone who'd do it for you?" said Ethel again, sweetly.

He thought for a minute.

"Well, I'm sure the curate wouldn't mind doing it," he said at last. "I've often taken his boys' club for him."

"Well, William could take the message to him, couldn't he?" said Ethel.

Glorious idea! It would kill two birds with

one stone. It would prolong this wonderful tête-à-tête and get rid of this objectionable boy.

Mr Solomon smiled upon William almost benignly.

"You'll do that, won't you, William?"

"Yes," said William obligingly, "cert'nly."

"Listen very carefully to me then, dear boy," said Mr Solomon. "Go to Mr Greene's house and ask him if he'd be kind enough to take over my duties for this afternoon as I'm – er – unable to attend to them myself. Tell him that the two sacks containing the gifts for the old folks' party and the mixed infants' party are in my rooms. The larger of the two is the old folks' party presents. He'll find in my rooms, too, a Father Christmas costume which he should wear for giving the old folks' presents, and a Pied Piper costume for giving the mixed infants' presents . . ."

William walked slowly down the road to Mr Solomon's rooms.

He had decided after all *not* to call upon

the curate. He had decided very kindly to perform Mr Solomon's two little duties himself.

He was most anxious to be admitted to Mr Solomon's band as a trumpeter, and he thought that if Mr Solomon found his two little duties correctly performed by William his heart might be melted and he might admit William as a trumpeter to his band.

Moreover, there is no denying that the thought of dressing up as Father Christmas and the Pied Piper and distributing gifts to old folks and mixed infants appealed very strongly indeed to William's highly developed dramatic instinct.

Mr Solomon's housekeeper admitted him without question and a few minutes later William staggered across to the school with two large sacks and two large bundles over his shoulders.

He found a small classroom to change in. It was intensely thrilling to put on the Father Christmas beard and wig and the trailing

red cloak edged with cotton wool.

He then carefully considered the two sacks. Why should the old folks have a larger sack than the mixed infants? he thought.

He shouldered the *smaller* sack therefore and set off to the old folks' party.

As he entered, old folks in various stages of old age sat round the room, talking to each other complainingly.

They were engaged in discussing among themselves the inadequacy of the tea, the uncomfortableness of the chairs, the piercingness of the draught, and the general dullness of the party.

"'Tisn't what it used to be in my young days," one old man was saying loudly to his neighbours.

At the sight of William with his sack they brightened.

A perspiring young man and woman hurried down to him eagerly.

"So glad to see you," they gasped. "You're awfully late – I suppose Mr Solomon sent you with the things?"

Not much of William's face could be seen through the beard and wig, but what could be seen signified assent.

"Well, do begin to give them out," said the young man. "It's simply ghastly! They won't do anything but sit round and grumble. I hope you've got plenty of tea and 'baccy. That's what they like best."

William began, and it was not until he had presented an outraged old man with a toy engine that it occurred to him that it had been perhaps a mistake to exchange the two sacks.

But having begun, he went doggedly on with his task.

He presented to the old men and women around him dolls and tin motor cars and little wooden boats and garish little picture books and pencil cases – all presents laboriously chosen by Mr Solomon for the mixed infants.

The old folks were amazed and indignant. But there was something of satisfaction in their indignation. Something fresh to grumble at was almost in the nature of a godsend.

William gathered from the homicidal expressions with which the helpers were watching him that it would be as well to retire as hastily as possible.

He handed his last present, a child's paintbox, to an old woman by the door and departed almost precipitately.

Then the storm broke out and a torrent of shrill indignation pursued his retreating form.

He changed into the Pied Piper costume, retaining his Father Christmas beard and wig in order to better conceal his identity.

Then he shouldered his other sack and a few moments later he flung open the door of a room in which a few dozen mixed infants gambolled half-heartedly at the bidding of their conscientious helpers.

A little cluster of mothers sat at the end of the room and watched them proudly.

The mixed infants, seeing him enter with his sack, brightened and broke into a thin shrill cheer. A helper came down to greet him.

"How good of you to come," she said gushingly. "The procession first, of course – the children know just what to do – we've been rehearsing it."

The mixed infants were already getting into line. The helper motioned William to the head of it.

"Twice round the room, you know," said the helper, "and then distribute the presents."

William began very slowly to walk round the room, his sack on his shoulder, his train of mixed infants prancing joyously behind.

William's brain was working quickly. He had a strong suspicion that he would soon be distributing packets of tea and tobacco to a gathering of outraged mixed infants.

His hopes of being admitted into Mr Solomon's band faded.

Then, suddenly, he decided not to await meekly the blows of fate. Instead he'd play a bold game.

The mothers and helpers were surprised

when suddenly William, followed by his faithful band, walked out of the door and disappeared from view.

But an intelligent helper smiled brightly and said, "How thoughtful! He's just going to take them once round the school outside. I expect quite a lot of people are hanging about hoping for a glimpse of them."

"Who is he?" said a mother. "I thought Mr Solomon was to have come."

"Oh, it's probably one of Mr Solomon's elder Sunday school boys. He told me once that he believed in training them up in habits of social service. He's a wonderful man. I'm sure he'd have come if some more pressing duty hadn't detained him. The dear man's probably reading to some poor invalid at this moment."

At that moment (as a matter of fact) the dear man had got to the point where he was earnestly informing Ethel that no one had ever, ever, ever understood him in all his life as she did.

It wasn't until several minutes later that frenzied mothers and helpers poured out into the playground. It was empty.

They poured out into the street. It was empty. Everything was empty.

The old legend had come true. A Pied Piper followed by every mixed infant had vanished completely from the face of the earth.

Ethel had just sneezed, and Mr Solomon was just thinking how much more musically she sneezed than anyone else he had ever met, when the mothers and helpers burst in upon them.

They took in the situation at a glance and never again did Mr Solomon recapture the pedestal from which that glance deposed him.

But the immediate question was the mixed infants.

"B-b-but Mr Greene came to give the presents," gasped Mr Solomon. "It was Mr Greene."

"It certainly wasn't Mr Greene," said a helper tartly, "it was a boy. We thought it must have been one of your Sunday school boys. We couldn't see his face plainly because of his beard."

A feeling of horror stole over Mr Solomon. With a crowd of distracted mothers at his heels he returned to the school and conducted a thorough and systematic search. No mixed infants. The attitude of the mothers was growing hostile. They evidently looked upon Mr Solomon as solely responsible for the calamity.

"Sittin' there," muttered a mother fiercely, "sittin' there dallyin' with red-haired females while our children was bein' stole – *Nero!*"

"*'Erod!*" said another, not to be outdone in general culture.

"*Crippen!*" said another showing herself more up-to-date.

The perspiration was pouring from Mr Solomon's brow. It was like a nightmare.

"I – I'll go and look round the village," he said desperately. "I'll go to the police – I promise I'll find them."

"You'd better," said someone darkly.

He tore in panic down the road. He tore in panic up the nearest street. And then, suddenly, he saw William's face looking at him over a garden gate.

"Hello," said William.

"Do you know anything about those children?" panted Mr Solomon.

"Yes," said William calmly. "If you'll promise to let me be a trumpeter in your band, you can have them. Will you?"

"Y–yes," spluttered Mr Solomon.

"On your honour?" persisted William.

"Yes," said Mr Solomon. "Yes—"

"An' Ginger an' Henry an' Douglas – all trumpeters?"

"Yes," said Mr Solomon desperately.

It was at that moment that Mr Solomon decided that not even Ethel's charm would compensate for having William for a brother-in-law.

"All right," said William, "come round here."

He led him round to a garage at the back of the house and opened the door.

The garage was full of mixed infants having the time of their lives, engaged in mimic warfare under the leadership of Ginger and Douglas with ammunition of tea-leaves and tobacco.

Certainly the mixed infants were appreciating the old folks' presents far more than the old folks had appreciated the mixed infants'.

"Here they are," said William carelessly,

"you can have 'em if you like. We're gettin' a bit tired of them."

No words of mine could describe the touching reunion between the mixed infants and their mothers.

Neither could any words of mine describe the first practice of Mr Solomon's Sunday school band with William, Ginger, Henry and Douglas as trumpeters.

There was, however, only one practice, as after that Mr Solomon wisely decided to go away for a very long holiday.

# William's New Year's Day

Mr Moss, who owned the village sweet-shop, handed a fruit drop to William. William received it gratefully.

"An' what good resolution are you going to take tomorrow?" said Mr Moss.

William crunched in silence for a minute, then, "Good resolution?" he questioned. "I ain't got none."

"You've got to have a good resolution for New Year's Day," said Mr Moss firmly.

William pondered.

"Can't think of anything," he said. "You think of somethin' for me."

"Well, you might take one to do your schoolwork properly."

William shook his head very firmly.

"Crumbs, no!"

"Or to be polite."

"P'lite?"

"Yes. 'Please' and 'thank you', and 'if you don't mind me sayin' so', and 'if you excuse me contradictin' of you', and 'can I do anything for you?' and such like."

William was struck with this.

"Yes, I might be that," he said. "Yes, I might try bein' that. How long has it to go on, though?"

"Not long," said Mr Moss. "Only the first day gen'rally. Folks gen'rally give 'em up after that."

"What's yours?" said William.

Mr Moss leant forward confidentially.

"I'm goin' to arsk 'er again," he said.

"Who?" said William, mystified.

"Someone I've arsked reg'lar every New Year's Day for ten year."

"Asked what?"

"Arsked to take me, o' course,"

"Take you where? Where d'you want to go? Why can't you go yourself?"

"Ter *marry* me, I means," said Mr Moss, blushing slightly as he spoke.

"Well," said William with a judicial air, "I wun't have asked the same one for ten years. I'd have tried someone else. You'd be sure to find someone that wouldn't mind you – with a sweet-shop, too. She must be a softie. Does she *know* you've got a sweet-shop?"

*

The next morning William leapt out of bed with an expression of stern resolve.

"I'm goin' to be p'lite," he remarked to his bedroom furniture. "I'm goin' to be p'lite all day."

He met his father on the stairs.

"Good mornin', Father," he said. "Can I do anythin' for you today?"

His father looked down at him suspiciously.

"What do you want now?" he demanded.

William was hurt.

"I'm only bein' p'lite. It's – you know – one of those things you take on New Year's Day. Well, I've took one to be p'lite."

His father apologised.

"I'm sorry. You see, I'm not used to it. It startled me."

After breakfast, William made his way to the sweet-shop.

Mr Moss was at the door, hatted and coated, and gazing anxiously down the street.

"Goo' mornin', Mr Moss," said William politely.

Mr Moss took out a large antique watch.

"He's late!" he said. "I shall miss the train. Oh, dear! It will be the first New Year's Day I've missed in ten years. Will you – will you do something for me and I'll *give* you a quarter of those new pink ones."

William gasped. The offer was almost too munificent to be true.

"I'll do *anythin'* for that," he said simply.

"Well, just stay in the shop till my nephew Bill comes. 'E'll be 'ere in two shakes, an' I'll miss my train if I don't go now. 'E's goin' to keep the shop for me till I'm back. You can weigh yourself a quarter o' those sweets."

William was left alone. The ideal of his childhood was realised. He had a sweet-shop.

He walked round the shop with a conscious swagger, pausing to pop a butter-ball into his mouth.

It was all his – all those rows and rows of

gleaming bottles of sweets of every size and colour, those boxes and boxes of attractively arranged chocolates.

He owned them all.

A small boy appeared in the doorway. William scowled at him.

"Well," he said ungraciously, "what d'you want?"

Then, suddenly remembering his Resolution, "*Please* what d'you want?"

"Where's Uncle?" said the small boy with equal ungraciousness. "'Cause our Bill's ill, an' can't come."

William waved him off.

"That's all right," he said. "You tell 'em that's all right. That's quite all right. See? Now, you go off!"

The small boy stood, as though rooted to the spot. William pressed into one of his hands a stick of liquorice and into the other a packet of chocolate.

"Now, you go *away*! I don't *want* you here. See?"

The small boy made off, clutching his spoils.

William called after the retreating figure, "If you don't mind me sayin' so."

He had already come to look upon the New Year's Resolution as a kind of god who must at all costs be propitiated.

Already the Resolution seemed to have bestowed upon him the dream of his life – a fully equipped sweet-shop.

A thin lady of uncertain age came in.

"Good morning," she said icily. "Where's Mr Moss?"

William answered as well as the presence of five sweets in his mouth would allow him.

"Gone," he said, then murmured vaguely, "thank you," as the thought of the Resolution loomed up in his mind.

"Who's in charge?"

"Me," said William.

She looked at him with distinct disapproval.

"Well, I'll have one of those bars of chocolate."

William, looking round the shop, realised suddenly there was a chance of making good any loss that Mr Moss might otherwise have sustained.

He looked down at the twopenny bars.

"Shillin' each," he said firmly.

She gasped.

"They were only twopence yesterday."

"They're gone up since, if you'll kin'ly 'scuse me sayin' so."

"Gone up—? Have you heard from the makers they're gone up?"

"Yes'm," said William politely.

"When did you hear?"

"This mornin' if you don't mind me sayin' so."

William's manner of fulsome politeness seemed to madden her.

"Did you hear by post?"

"Yes'm. By post this mornin'."

She glared at him with vindictive triumph.

"I happen to live opposite, you wicked lying boy, and I know that the postman did not call here this morning."

William met her eye calmly.

"No, they came round to see me in the night – the makers did. You cou'n't of heard them," he added hastily. "It was when you was asleep. If you'll 'scuse me contradictin' of you."

It is a great gift to be able to lie so as to convince other people. It is a still greater gift to be able to lie so as to convince yourself.

William was possessed of the latter gift.

"I shall certainly not pay more than twopence," said his customer severely, taking a bar of chocolate and laying down twopence on the counter. "And I shall report this shop to the Profiteering Committee. It's scandalous."

William scowled at her.

"They're a *shillin'*," he said. "I don't want your nasty ole tuppences. I said they was a *shillin'*."

He followed her to the door. She was crossing the street to her house. "You – you ole *thief*!" he yelled after her, though, true to his Resolution, he added softly with dogged determination, "if you don't mind me sayin' so."

He was next disturbed by the entry of another customer. Swallowing a nutty football whole, he hastened to his post behind the counter.

The newcomer was a dainty little girl of about nine – dressed in a white fur coat and cap and long white gaiters.

William had seen this vision on various occasions in the town, but had never yet addressed it.

He smiled – a self-conscious, sheepish smile – as she came up to the counter.

"Please, I want two twopenny bars of chocolate."

She laid four pennies on the counter.

"You can have lots for that," said William huskily. "An' – what else would you like?"

"Please, I haven't any more money," gasped a small, bewildered voice.

"*Money* don't matter," said William. "Things is cheap today. You can have – anythin' you like for that fourpence. Anythin' you like."

"'Cause it's New Year's Day?" said the vision, with a gleam of understanding.

"Yes," said William, "'cause it's that."

"Is it your shop?"

"Yes," said William with an air of importance. "It's all my shop. You take anythin' you like."

She collected as much as she could carry and started towards the door. "*Sank* you! Sank you ever so!" she said gratefully.

"It's all right," said William with an indulgent smile. "Not at all. Don't menshun it. Not at all. Quite all right."

He bowed with would-be gracefulness as she went through the doorway.

As she passed the window, she stopped and kissed her hand.

William blinked with pure emotion.

Then, absent-mindedly, crammed his mouth with a handful of mixed dewdrops.

As he crunched he caught sight of two of his friends flattening their noses at the window. He went to the door.

They gazed at him in wonder.

"I've got a shop," he said casually. "Come on in an' look at it."

They entered, open-mouthed. They gazed at the boxes and bottles of sweets. Aladdin's Cave was nothing to this.

"How'd you get it, William?" gasped Ginger.

"Someone gave it me," said William. "I took one of them things to be p'lite, and someone gave it to me. Go on, jus' help yourselves. Not at all. Jus' help yourselves an' don't menshun it."

They needed no second bidding.

They went from box to box, putting handfuls of sweets and chocolates into their mouths. They said nothing, because speech was a physical impossibility.

A close observer might have noticed that William now ate little.

William himself had been conscious for some time of a curious and inexplicable feeling of coldness towards the tempting dainties around him.

He was, however, loath to give in to the weakness, and every now and then he nonchalantly put into his mouth a toasted square or a fruity bit.

It happened that a loutish boy of about

fourteen was passing the shop. At the sight of three small boys rapidly consuming the contents, he became interested.

"What yer doin'?" he said indignantly, standing in the doorway.

"You get out of my shop," said William valiantly.

"*Yer* shop?" said the boy. "Yer bloomin' well pinchin' things out o' someone else's shop. 'Ere, gimme some of them."

"You get *out*!" said William.

"Get out *yerself*!" said the other.

"If I'd not took one to be p'lite," said William threateningly, "I'd knock you down."

"Yer would, would yer?" said the other, beginning to roll up his sleeves.

"Yes, I would, too. You get out."

Seizing the nearest bottle, which happened to contain acid drops, William began to fire them at his opponent's head. One hit him in the eye. He retired into the street. William followed him, still hurling acid drops with all his might.

A crowd of boys collected together. Some gathered acid drops from the gutter, others joined the scrimmage.

William, Henry and Ginger carried on a noble fight against heavy odds.

It was only the sight of the proprietor of the shop coming briskly down the sidewalk that put an end to the battle.

The street boys made off in one direction and Ginger and Henry in another. William, clasping an empty acid drop bottle to his bosom, was left to face Mr Moss.

Mr Moss entered and looked round with an air of bewilderment.

"Where's Bill?" he said.

"He's ill," said William. "He couldn't come. I've been keepin' shop for you. I've done the best I could."

He looked round the rifled shop anxiously. But Mr Moss hardly seemed to notice.

"Thanks, William," he said almost humbly. "William, she's took me. She's goin' ter marry me. Isn't it grand? After all these years."

"I'm afraid there's a bit of a mess," said William.

Mr Moss waved aside his apologies.

"It doesn't matter, William," he said. "Nothing matters today. She's took me at last. I'm goin' to shut shop this afternoon and go over to her again. Thanks for staying, William."

"Not at all. Don't menshun it," said William nobly. Then, "I think I've had enough of that bein' p'lite. Will one mornin' do for this year, d'you think?"

"Er – yes. Well, I'll shut up. Don't you stay, William. You'll want to be getting home for lunch."

Lunch? Quite definitely William decided that he did not want any lunch.

The very thought of lunch brought with it a feeling of active physical discomfort, which was much more than mere absence of hunger.

He decided to go home as quickly as possible, though not to lunch.

"Goo'bye," he said.

"Goodbye," said Mr Moss.

"I'm afraid you'll find some things gone," said William faintly. "Some boys was in."

"That's all right, William," said Mr Moss, roused again from his rosy dreams. "That's quite all right."

But it was not "quite all right" with William.

If you had been left, at the age of eleven, in sole charge of a sweet-shop for a whole morning, would it have been "all right" with you? No.

But we will not follow William through the humiliating hours of the afternoon. We will leave him pale and unsteady, but for now master of the situation, as he wends his homeward way.

Meet Just William
**Richmal Crompton**
**Adapted by Martin Jarvis**
**Illustrated by Tony Ross**

*Just William as you've never seen him before!*

A wonderful new series of *Just William* books, each containing four of his funniest stories – all specially adapted for younger readers by Martin Jarvis, the famous "voice of William" on radio and best-selling audio cassette.

Meet Just William and the long-suffering Brown family, as well as the Outlaws, Violet Elizabeth Bott and a host of other favourite characters in these ten hilarious books.

1. William's Birthday and Other Stories
2. William and the Hidden Treasure and Other Stories
3. William's Wonderful Plan and Other Stories
4. William and the Prize Cat and Other Stories
5. William's Haunted House and Other Stories
6. William's Day Off and Other Stories

Richmal Crompton
**Just William at Christmas**

Christmas is a time for peace, joy and goodwill. But William's presence has never been known to enhance the spirit of the season.

Whether he's wrecking the Sunday School's carol singing outing, standing in as Santa Claus for the Old Folk, or making a Christmas plant pot out of Ethel's hat, William somehow manages to spread chaos wherever he goes.

Ten unforgettable stories of William at Christmas, with the original illustrations by Thomas Henry.